This book belongs to:

_____

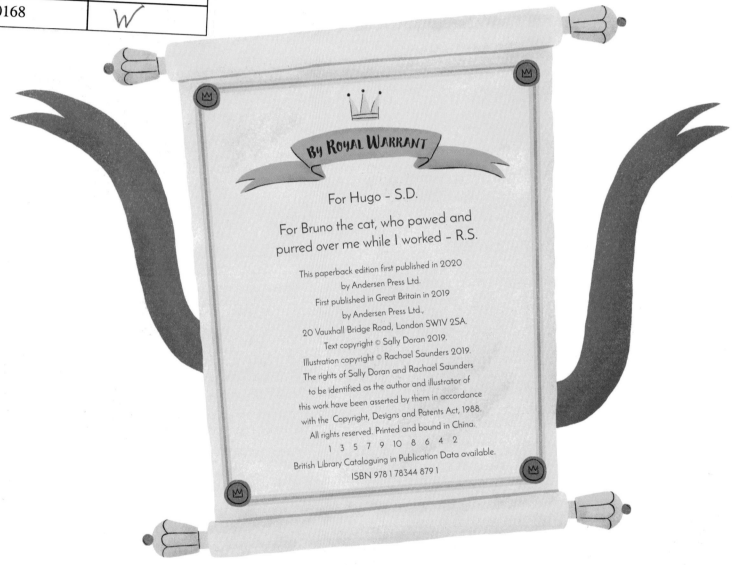

By Royal Warrant

For Hugo - S.D.

For Bruno the cat, who pawed and
purred over me while I worked - R.S.

This paperback edition first published in 2020
by Andersen Press Ltd.
First published in Great Britain in 2019
by Andersen Press Ltd.,
20 Vauxhall Bridge Road, London SW1V 2SA.
Text copyright © Sally Doran 2019.
Illustration copyright © Rachael Saunders 2019.
The rights of Sally Doran and Rachael Saunders
to be identified as the author and illustrator of
this work have been asserted by them in accordance
with the Copyright, Designs and Patents Act, 1988.
All rights reserved. Printed and bound in China.
1 3 5 7 9 10 8 6 4 2
British Library Cataloguing in Publication Data available.
ISBN 978 1 78344 879 1

BOOM! BANG! Royal Meringue!

Sally Doran

Rachael Saunders

ANDERSEN PRESS

Young Princess Hannah grew up in a palace
with her father King Monty and mother Queen Alice.

She always said "thank you" and "pardon" and "please".
She ate all her cabbage and parsnips and peas.
"I'm ever so proud," said the King to his wife.
"She's the finest young lady I've met in my life!"

The Queen quite agreed,
so they planned it together:
their daughter deserved
the best birthday ever!

"Happy birthday my dear, what a day!" said the King. "We've bought you this marvellous, wonderful thing!"

She ripped off the paper
and pulled off the bow.
"What is it?" she asked.
"Why, my dear, don't you know?"

it had
hundreds of
dials and
switches
and knobs.

It was big,
it was gold,
it had
buttons
and cogs,

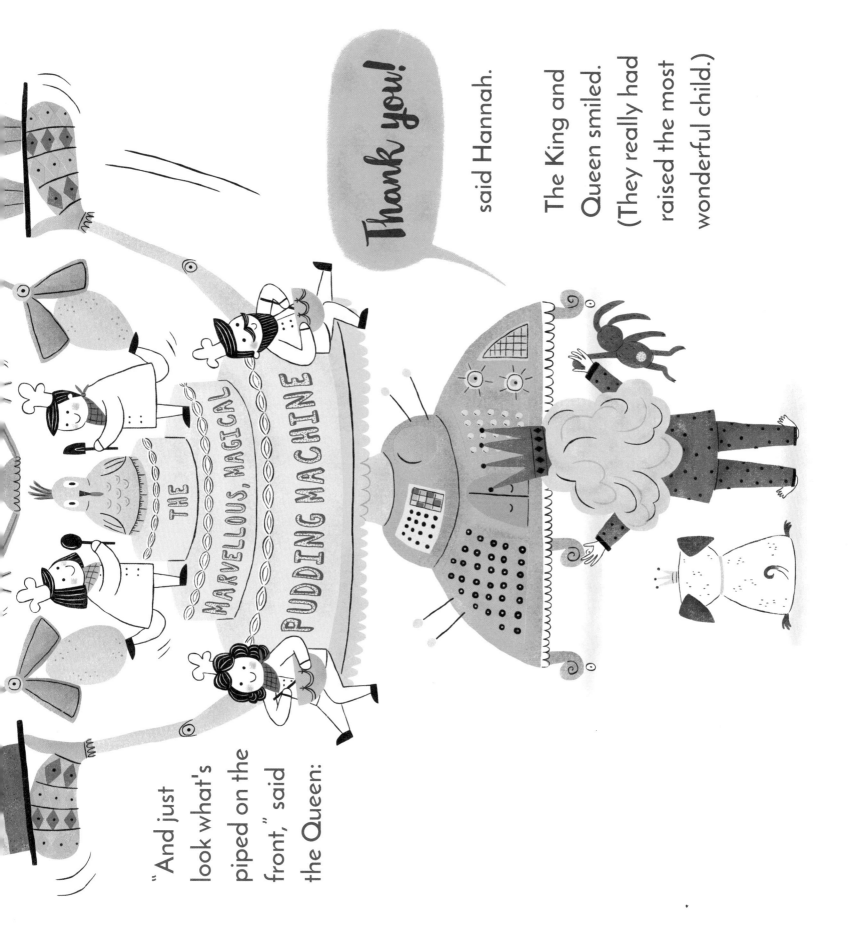

"And just look what's piped on the front," said the Queen:

THE MARVELLOUS, MAGICAL PUDDING MACHINE

Thank you!

said Hannah.

The King and Queen smiled. (They really had raised the most wonderful child.)

That evening they threw her
a big birthday ball
in the palace's fabulous
banqueting hall.

Every young person from
far and from wide was invited
to dine by the Princess's side.

"Well, now that the party is in full swing, bring forth the Pudding Machine," said the King.

So the big gold machine was wheeled into view to the sounds of

WOW! and **LOOK!** and **OOH!**

The Princess played with the buttons and knobs. She spun all the dials and turned all the cogs.

With a **boom** and a **pop** bright sparks filled the air...

and out shot a glorious chocolate *éclair!*

Then with a
CRASH
and a **bang** and a **fizzle**...

out shot a pudding with caramel drizzle.

"Well done, my dear," said the King. "What a show! Now why don't we let all your friends have a go?"

THE MARVELLOUS, MAGICAL ...DING MACHINE

But the Princess
climbed down
straight away
and said...

No!

"That present is mine!"
the young royal howled
and she threw her tiara
and pouted and scowled.

She thumped her fists and stamped on the floor
and threw all her puddings and cakes at the door.

"Something's quite wrong — she's ill!" the King said,
as a bowl of rice pudding sailed right past his head.

"No," said the Queen,
brushing cream from her hair.
"It seems we've forgotten
to teach her to share."

"But hang on a minute – whatever is that?"

BOOM!
Bang!
Thumpety-splat!

The young guests were giving
the buttons a bang,
till out shot a huge pie
with blackbirds that **sang!**

The crowd said "Goodness!"
and "My, what a thing!"
And the Princess stopped crying
and smiled at the King.

Just look at that **pie!**
Wait for me!

Hannah said,
as she pushed her tiara
back onto her head.

She played
with her friends,
and to her surprise,
together they made
better puddings and pies!

A jelly appeared with a
BOOM and a **POP**,
with fireworks shooting
right out of the top.

Then out flew a pudding
shaped like a boat
and a gingerbread castle
complete with a moat.

The big gold machine then **coughed, shook** and **spluttered.**

"Good gracious - it's bulging," the King and Queen muttered.

With a **BOOM** and a **BANG** came a sparkling pink cloud and a hush spread through all the guests in the crowd...

For a **GIANT** meringue
almost 20 feet tall
now sat on the floor
of the banqueting hall.

The crowd all cheered.
"Well perhaps we should eat,"
said the Queen to the King
as she got to her feet.

"Fetch some meringue," said the King. "Ah yes, and some cream and some berries, we'll have **Eton Mess!**"

So straight up the sugary face Hannah sped
and carved out some pieces as big as her head!

A wonderful time was had by them all,
as **laughter** and **joy** filled the banqueting hall.

"Just look at the time, it's late!" the King said.
"It's time Princess Hannah was off to her bed."
So she thanked all her guests
and curtsied and bowed.
"What a **charming** princess she is,"
said the crowd.

From that moment Hannah
was good as can be,
always sharing her cakes
when her friends came to tea.

And as for the meringue? Well, from what I hear,
to eat the whole thing took the Kingdom a year!